"GOD, the Lord, is my strength; he makes my feet like the deer's; he makes me tread on my high places."
~ Habakkuk 3:19

~ Anya vondersuft

2

ICE BOMB

The Exciting Adventures of Two Loyal Friends
And their Cunning Dog, Tardis!!

Other Books by Anya vonderLuft

Thoughts on the Theme of Life

The Magical Keystone

Biblical Femininity

The Best Poems

ICE BOMB

Copyright © 2019 Anya vonderLuft
All rights reserved. No part of this book may be reproduced, stored in a retrieval system, or transmitted in any form or by any means – electronic, mechanical, photocopy, recording, or otherwise –except for brief quotations for the purpose of review or comment without the prior permission of the publisher, lulu.com

Printed in the United States of America
Science Fiction
Ist Edition

vonderLuft, Anya 1985–

Dedicated to Kurtis Bradley and Malcolm Anderson

8

Kurtis kicked angrily at the rocks in front of him as he walked to the old house. The stone walkway was quiet, with only the dust and dirt from his feet, rising from the ground. The California summer was hotter and drier than normal, causing a slight drought and the sun caused a very deep sunburn almost instantaneously. He wished that he still had his trusty old road bike, but the wheels were busted and the fender was a terrible wreck, due to a dare from his old friend, Malcolm. He had received his bike for his birthday, a while back and was fond of taking it out in wild blue yonder to go exploring and visit the unknown.
"Man, that was such a blast, last year, though!" he remembered with a big grin on his face.

He started to get gloomy again, as he remembered that there was an awful reason why he was walking so far on this beautiful Saturday morning. His brother, James, was on a Camping Trip, so he still had to wash the fence. James was camping in the beautiful Cascade Mountain range. He had a tent, a sleeping bag, some dried and fresh food, and a lot of other neat camping gear. Malcolm was a little envious of him and wished that he could experience something exciting. He hurriedly got a pail and some whitewash and started scrubbing the fence. It was taking too long. The fence was really dirty and the work of scrubbing it was extremely tiring. Malcolm thought that by the time that he was done, more whitewash was on him, than on the fence. He wasn't sure if that was a good thing or a bad thing. He took the pail to the shed and put it back where it belonged. Then he went to the house to clean himself up.

Kurtis and Malcolm were close friends and because of this, at some point, there was bound to be trouble. That is just what happened. Little did they know that something terrible was about to happen!

Kurtis ran to the shed. It was an old rickety shed. His grandfather had built it a long time ago. Some of the boards were rotted through and the paint was dry and cracked. Malcolm, the adventurous one, was eager to find out what was inside and whether or not, a special treasure was incased down in the depths. Young men love the thought of buried treasure and pirates and treasure tend to excite them a lot. He asked Kurtis to go find a tool to pick the rusty lock that was holding the dilapidated door shut tight. Kurtis was sure that they would be able to find the gold easily. Then he would grab it, put it all into his pouch, run away, and take on the adventure of a lifetime. The day after he left,

Malcolm ran over to the shed, opened it, and looked inside to see if what he said was true. Malcolm had a magic key that would accomplish amazing feats with just the snap of a finger. He wanted the treasure for himself and his friend was too cautious to even think of going on this adventure alone. The shed was so dark and he didn't have any light. Malcolm groped around for awhile, but soon he lost his interest. He suddenly remembered about Kurtis. Where was he? What had happened? He got tired of searching and left to go to his house. Kurtis still had not come back. Malcolm started to get worried. Why was his friend taking so long? He had sent him on a simple task to go find the key to the shed. Even though it seemed kind of boring, who would pass up anything that had to do with finding buried treasure or better yet genuine gems? Malcolm opened the door to his house. He took off his coat and went into the kitchen to see if he could find something to eat. His dog, Tardis, ran to meet him and jumped up to lick his face. Malcolm stroked the dog thoughtfully and went to find some food for him. He wondered if the dog sensed something strange. There was a strange feel and smell to the house and he wondered what it was. Tardis rubbed his body against his master's face and looked up at him with eager eyes. Malcolm started to get suspicious. He looked around. His house was a mess. There were things all over the floor, his desk drawers were open and his tools were all gone. One of the windows was cracked and the shelves were almost empty. What if Kurtis had got mad when he had directed him to go on that mission alone to retrieve the key to the shed? Malcolm had already unlocked it and looked thoroughly inside to see if any treasure was to be found, but there was nothing. It probably served him right. The reality was that Tardis had tramped in when neither of them were looking in order to search for his stash of bones that he was planning to hide in a secret place outdoors.

As for Kurtis, he found himself dealing with a totally different problem. It was a new experience for him, and he was a little frightened at the same time. After Malcolm had sent him off to find the key, Kurtis went back to the house. Malcolm didn't find him because Kurtis had discovered a most distinctive dilapidated rusty trap door. His house was very spacious and there were many nooks and crannies where he would keep all of the treasures that he and Malcolm had found over the years when they went on their hikes and adventures. Kurtis opened the trap door to look around. It was dark, so he couldn't see very well. He suddenly stumbled over something hard. He heard a queer voice and he felt an object grab him and start to pull him forward. The grip was strong. He struggled to get free, but it was no use. He screamed for help, but there was nothing. The object started to pull him with full force toward the opening of the trap door. He couldn't see, and outside the trap door, it was totally dark. He wished his dog, Tardis, were with him. His dog would have barked loudly and tried to wrestle and destroy the invisible thing, whatever it was, but he was nowhere to be found. Tardis was adventurous, cunning, and daring like his master. As soon as Tardis heard him scream, he shot off like a cheetah and hid under the shade of a large tree near Malcolm's house.

    Meanwhile Kurtis continued to feel the strong grip between his attacker and himself. He started to experience sharp pains and felt himself being whirled around faster than a tornado. The beauty of the California sun, the trees, and all of the things at his house disappeared. He could hardly see anything at all. Before he knew it, the planet earth was behind him and he was thrust into the dark unknown and the wondrous spaciousness of the Milky Way Galaxy. He did not have any astronomical gear and he had lost all of his possessions while being thrust into the unknown. The temperature was so cold and he felt colder than ice. Meteors and meteorites flew past him so fast that he thought that he was going to be crushed with a forcefull blow. He began to think that he was only an illusion and that it was not himself at all. He lost all sense of reality. The world seemed dark and hazy to him. How could someone live in the vast solar system without the comfort of the planet earth and the beautiful green trees, flowers, oxygen, and ultimately life? The whole thing was totally crazy. Why had Malcolm been so mean as to send him on that mission alone, even though it was a small one, when he knew all along how to get into the secret place and search for the wonderful treasure of his imagination? The treasure probably didn't even exist. He didn't realize it at first, but soon he knew he had been tricked. When Kurtis didn't come back with the key, Malcolm started to feel a little uneasy himself. He sat down for a while to think things over. Now it was too late. The treasure was gone and he was gone too. Malcolm didn't know how long he had been sitting there thinking, but before he knew it, he heard a loud noise. The noise kept getting louder and louder. Soon he found himself lifted high in the air and being pulled along by an unseen force.

    The air was so stale that he could hardly breathe. Like Kurtis, he soon lost all sense of reality. It felt colder than ice and he was blue with cold. Was he in another realm? The whole atmosphere was totally dark. Suddenly another form appeared very close to him. That form was his friend, Kurtis. He was wearing some sort of white suit. It was very bulky and on the back of it, there was some sort of pack. The atmosphere and grounds were totally red. It was a very dark red and there were rocks and debris everywhere. What was this lonely red world; a world that was −195 degrees F? During this adventure, winter had come so fast.

They were now stranded on the planet, Mars. They looked around. Everything was empty. There was no life, and Tardis was nowhere to be seen. With no food or water, they needed to do something quickly, but what could they do? It is extremely difficult to survive in weather that is -195 degrees F. Kurtis whispered to Malcolm and they pulled a long role of electrical tape out of his new survival pack. He thought that they could insulate themselves with it. On the way to this uninhabited galaxy, Kurtis had tried to grab anything that he could reach while being tossed and hurled through the air at the speed of light.

There was one small way to fix part of the problem about food. After Kurtis saw that Malcolm had ended up on this tantalizing, freezing, red world, he pulled an apple out of his space pack. This was no ordinary apple and after he removed it from his pack, it swelled to enormous size. He had hurriedly painted it with what he called paint, but was actually colored caramel. Malcolm thought that it had turned blue due to the weather that was many degrees below freezing. He looked at it with surprise.

"What have you done? How did that happen," he ejaculated? Kurtis broke a piece of it, the best he could in this extremely freezing weather. Out in the vastness of space, the darkness was over whelming, so it was extremely fortunate that this enormous caramel apple glowed in the dark. Before either of them could even take a bite, an enormous monster immerged from the thick dark red atmosphere.

It had scales like a fish and teeth like a shark. Out of the sides of its mouth, hung two large fangs like giant sabers. It had large pointed spines on his back like that of a dinosaur. His feet were like the feet of a grizzly bear and it breathed fire like a dragon. He also had bat wings and could fly extremely well. Kurtis and Malcolm were terrified. They started to get a little bit angry. Why did James have the comforts and joys of a camping trip, when they were having an exciting moment of hunting for buried treasure and suddenly were thrust into a dark cold red demon world? It was a world that was creepy, scary, and adventurous.

However, it was kind of exciting as well and they didn't know, but they would be stuck on this planet and doomed to stay in this unknown freezing world for the rest of their lives. The monster rose from its place with a steaming roar and a voice like the great Darth Vador of old times. Its footsteps shook the red planet and forced it to spin so fast that Kurtis and Malcolm were nearly crushed and thrown down into the depths of the whole universe. The monster shouted as though he knew them and what they had done.

"WHY HAVE YOU INVADED MY TERRITORY? NOW THAT YOU HAVE DONE SO, YOU WILL FOREVER BE MY SUBJECTS. GET RID OF ALL HOPES THAT YOU HAVE OF GETTING BACK TO YOUR WORLD, IF THERE EVEN IS SUCH A PLACE. LET IT BE KNOWN TO YOU THAT YOU HAVE FAILED ME FOR THE LAST TIME.

When they heard these dreadful words, Kurtis and Malcolm became greatly afraid. What would life look like if they were stranded on the planet, Mars, for the rest of their lives? So many questions began to form in their minds. How could they have failed him, if they had never met him before? They started to look back at the past and think about what had transpired. First of all, they were two friends who had set out on an adventure to look for buried treasure in their

Grandfather's shed. One of them had gone inside to look around, but found nothing. The other one was sent off into the middle of nowhere to find an implement to look for what was supposed to be buried treasure, while his friend went to look for it himself. The result was that one ended up in a devastating position, while the other one, as though being punished for what he did, was thrust into the same position or worse. They had lost their trusty dog, which was probably whimpering, barking, and growling because his master had abandoned him. Oh, the horror. What an awful thought.

What had really happened to Tardis? Well, unlike his masters, Tardis was no ordinary dog. After the time when he pretended to be afraid by hiding under a tree and after his masters had disappeared, Tardis watched them go. After they were gone, he ran down into the shed where Malcolm started to look for the special treasure. Tardis had a very great imagination and you should not underestimate his ability to find treasure and hoard it for himself. It may be, that he would end up being smarter than them and take the treasure for himself. With his smart doggy mind, Tardis got to thinking really hard. That shed of their Grandfather's contained loads of magic powers. Tardis went down to inspect his stash of bones. The bones had been there for a couple years and during that time the powers of magic had doomed them to their fate. Tardis sniffed around inside the shed, as if he didn't remember where he had put them. There were a lot of different things in Grandfather's shed. A lot of them were old and rusty. There were things that had been handed down, pieces of wood, tools, toys, and various different kinds of gadgets. Hidden under some of the pieces of wood, there was a huge pile of bones, which Tardis had put there for safe keeping, just in case Malcolm, Kurtis, and James experienced a massive drought and famine, not that Malcolm and Kurtis could actually eat them.

Tardis looked around for a bit and then started digging fast and furiously. Deep down underneath a pile of rubble, there was a massive stash of beef bones. He had buried them long ago when Kurtis and Malcolm were out hunting for things to take pictures of. He started to inspect them as if he didn't think they were still good. During their long stay in the shed, Tardis's giant stash of bones had expanded to enormous size and not only that they had petrified into solid Gold.

Tardis was astonished and dumbfounded. Like Kurtis and Malcolm, he sat down and went into deep thought.

Years on Mars are massively different than a year on planet earth. While Tardis was still a spry young dog, his masters, had come of age faster than the blink of an eye. Besides being stranded on a freezing cold planet, their hair had turned so white that you could barely see it in the vastness of that cold land. If Tardis could see them now, he would not have been able to recognize them, much less see them at all. These bones that he had buried had contracted magic powers and when he was finally able to retrieve one from the shed, the moment that he touched it, he, the famous dog, Tardis, became aerodynamic. He gained the ability to fly. He knew that with this newly found power, he would be able to find his masters pretty quickly. Tardis became really excited. He took his stash of golden bones, tossed them onto his back, and bounded off in hot pursuit. He came to the edge of a cliff and prepared for blast off. With his stash of golden bones, he could not only fly but he could survive very well in the hottest or coldest climates that were spread throughout the universe. He prepared for action. It was the quest to save his masters from death, bring them back, and then go searching for the lost waif who they had left on a camping trip.

His stash of golden bones was so large and weighty that it only took two of them to accomplish his ascent. The weightiness of the bones would prevent him from blasting off, but the golden bones were magic and if Tardis told them to do something, the result would immediately be accomplished. It was time to go. 3 – 2 – 1 BLAST OFF! Tartis was amazed at how well he could fly. The golden bones allowed him to propel a lot faster than the speed of light. He was sure that he would be able to reach the planet Mars in no time, but he had a scary thought. His masters had been gone for so long and it was so cold on that desolate planet that they could be dead by now. It would be so horrible if he got to Mars, only to find that they were only skeleton fossils under sheets of solid ice that was 175 degrees below zero. Tartis zoomed past the planet, earth, in a moment of time. Before he knew it, he had landed on the planet Mars. Just as he feared, the planet was red, freezing cold, and barren of life. His masters, Kurtis and Malcolm were nowhere to be seen. A year on Mars is very different from a year on the planet earth. Tartis was crestfallen.

He didn't know about the horrendous monster that had tried to enslave them because they had invaded his Ice City. But he didn't care about these things at the moment. He was on the quest to find his master and rescue him and his friend from sudden death, with the assistance of his magic Golden Bones. Tartis had exactly 365 golden bones. There was one for each day of the year. He also had another one that was Silver for every four years when there was a Leap year. Tartis was absolutely sure that fresh bones were the cure for everything, and when they turned to gold, they were extra special and powerful. Perhaps his magic Golden Bones would be able to lead the way to Kurtis and Malcolm, or what he assumed was left of them. Tartis put a spell over his golden bones and told them to go find his masters, Kurtis and Malcolm. He barked at them and told them quite forcefully that if they were not able to lead him to his masters, than they would be cursed and banished to the land of the Alligator Dog, who would destroy their magic powers and crush their bone lives forever. The Alligator Dog was a horrible creature that terrorized man and beast, crushing their bones and invading their territory. Alligator dogs were also found on other planets and their presence there was just as frightening or more so, than if you were to encounter them on earth. This dog lived way down in the depths of the planet earth. The Golden Bones had a mind of their own and would not allow that to happen if they could help it.

Tartis looked around for what seemed to be a long time, sniffing and pawing the frozen ground. His Golden Bones were in a safe place stacked up neatly in a snow mound that he had dug out in this frozen land. It wasn't long before Tartis saw two tall ghostlike figures walking towards him. Their appearance was that of a whitish blue mist. Each of them were carrying an ice sword and an ice chest which was full of special ice proof gold coins along with a magic gem that was supposed to be able to help them get back to the planet earth.

Tartis didn't know what to think at first, but he was a smart dog and kept his eye on those ghostlike forms. He sensed there was something very suspicious and special about them, but what was it?

Tartis went up to the ghostlike forms and tried to paw at them. He wanted to undo their ghostly appearance if it was possible. At first, it seemed like there was nothing he could do. Ghosts do not have bodily forms. Then Tardis remembered his golden bones. He ran over to the pile and picked one up with his sharp teeth. He produced a sharp Ghostly Growl. "GRRRRUMPHWHOOOO"

The golden bones immediately went to work. It was like they became alive. One by one they traversed up to the ghost like figures and touched them at various points. As soon as this happened, the figures started to come to life. The misty halo disappeared and the ghostly forms disintegrated. Tardis was a little frightened and wondered if the bone magic would bring the desired effect. It did!

Before he knew it, the ghostliness was gone and two drenched human figures were facing him. At first he thought that they would freeze again, but the golden bones had multiple powers. They kept the humans warm at just the right temperature so that they would be able to make the flight back to earth. Tardis was ready for action now. When he saw that his master had come back to life, he rejoiced with multiple loud barks, but the temperature was freezing cold and there was no time to lose. If he were careful, his mouth would freeze open. That would be a disaster.

It was time to go home now. Their stay in this ice-cold world had gone on long enough, but first they had to deal with the ice monster who had threatened to enslave them for trespassing on his territory. Tardis's Golden Bones had powers to destroy monsters and so Tardis set right to work. As soon as the sound of the monster was heard, he talked to the Golden Bones. They sent out fiery sabers that choked the monster and sliced off his enormous head with one single blow. Now that the monster was dead, what would they do with him? How would they dispose of him and not freak people out. If anyone else decided to take the exciting adventure of going to another planet, whether accidently or on purpose, they would have to accept the challenge of discovering extraordinary dangers and treasures for themselves.

After the monster had died, Kurtis and Malcolm began to discuss how they would get back to earth. They had experienced the adventure of a lifetime and they would never forget it. They were so sorry that James had missed out on the fun. They decided that they would have to tell him about it when they got back. Kurtis set his dial to teleport back to earth at the Speed of Light. He pressed a magic button that was assisted by the help of the magic golden bones, and before they knew it, they were on their way back to the beautiful green life giving land; the Planet Earth. It was amazing how short the amount of time was that it took to get back to the planet, earth. They decided that they would hold onto each other's hands with Tardis and his magic bones, flying behind them. The magic bones needed to stay safe because they were the guarantee that would get them home and back to the green land and beautiful flowers that they loved so well. They knew that Tardis was really the one who had saved the day and they wanted to reward him when they all got back to earth. Before they knew it, the planet earth was in site. Their landing was spectacular. In some ways, they thought that it was more extraordinary then when they first started out. The return journey did not require a Space Craft, because the Magic Golden Beef Bones had accomplished their mission. All of the ordinary things on earth were not comparable to the adventure that they had experienced on the planet, Mars, the Red Planet. It was a miracle that they had survived. For a while, everything seemed a bit strange. They saw Kurtis's house where the adventure had started, they saw grandfather's shed where Tardis had uncovered his stash of Magic bones. Everything that had happened, now felt like a dream. Kurtis and Malcolm were true to their word and rewarded Tardis for saving their lives from the icy world and the Monster of Doom.

They told James and the rest of their friends all about their adventure. James was taken aback and at first, he thought it was just a joke. A camping trip is a lot more boring than a Space Mission, especially if it is a mission that involves dogs, monsters, cold red ice bomb planets and so much more. Before long they were in the newspaper. The Headline read, "TWO MEN SURVIVE ADVENTURE ON MARS. TRUSTY DOG TARDIS SAVES THEIR LIVES."

For many months, that was all that people talked about. They were quite taken about what Tardis had done. Some of them didn't believe the story and just thought that Kurtis and Malcolm's imaginations were running away with them. They were the talk of the town. It was a phenomenal adventure and accomplishment. The adventures of Kurtis, Malcolm, and Tardis were never to be forgotten. Could there really be life on the planet, Mars. People have different opinions. Is there life on Mars? Well, that is another story. Wait and see.

THE END

Acknowledgements:

Special Thanks to these Christian Friends for helping me out. Feedback from my editor, Ashley Bleoaja, and Kurtis Bradley who inspired me to rise beyond my expectations and write this book. Without his inspiration and encouragement, this would not have been possible. Thank you so much, my friends.

30

31